The Journey Of Transformation

BY

Neeraj Kumar

 pencil

ISBN 978-93-5438-950-4
© Neeraj Kumar 2021
Published in India 2021 by Pencil

A brand of
One Point Six Technologies Pvt. Ltd.
123, Building J2, Shram Seva Premises,
Wadala Truck Terminal, Wadala (E)
Mumbai 400037, Maharashtra, INDIA
E connect@thepencilapp.com
W www.thepencilapp.com

Author biography

A yogi, an engineer, a science enthusiast, and a vairagi. Discovering the unlimited source of energy which is claimed to be his.

Contents

Acknowledgements

In writing this book, I have drawn so much on the work of other linguists that a few if any of my ideas, except perhaps any mistaken ones, are original with me. I thank Sadhguru, Dale Carnegie, Steve Jobs, and Brandon Burchard for helping me through my rough times which inspired me to write a book for myself for future if in case I would need the help again. I thank my family to nurture me with the delicious foods and love.

Thanks to my friends at work, Siddharth Hota, Ankit Chaudhary, and Ashok Shehrawat, who has gone through my long list of questionnaire, and unknowingly helped me to write this book. Thanks to the friends with whom I travel the most, Ayushi Gupta, Nishant Sharma, Pooja Gupta, Somya Goyal and Khyati Agarwal, for being there with me in my ups and downs. Thanks to my another friend from work and college, Manisha Sharma, who inspired me to inspire her that if I can write the book so can she.

And here comes my college buddies, Akshay Kumar, Nitin Kumar, and Nitin Pal, I thank them for canceling all the trips 99% of the time, and that's at the end moment. I am proud of you my buuooyyss... I thank myself for maintaining the perseverance, patience, dedication, and for completing my first book in time.

I thank my bhole, my bhandari, one and only my Mahadev for keeping me alive, and for giving me everything that I may ask for, and that's without even asking him.

Now everyone say,

|| Har Har Mahadev ||

MAHADEV

The coolest and amazing personality in the entire universe. The more I say about him, the less it feels. He is everywhere and yet nowhere. He is within you and you're within him. He has no attachment with this world, and yet he is always there for the world, whether the world asks for him or not. He is the lord of the lords. He is away from this duality. He is neither good nor bad, god nor evil. Whether you believe in him or not, it doesn't matter to him. He is always there sitting in his meditative state, looking after this world. Don't try to find him, only recognize. Without his teachings, guidance and grace, I wouldn't be able to finish this book. All of what I had written in this book has been inspired from this timeless being in one way or the other.

May Mahadev will help you throughout this journey ofself-transformation.

"Only reciting my name isn't enough, actions are also necessary." ~Mahadev

|| Har Har Mahadev ||

INTRODUCTION

Are you confused about what to do in life? There is no peace of mind. Are you afraid to choose a single path to walk on? You have heard a lot about finding passion, and you are still unable to find it. Have you lost hope in almost everything around you? Nothing tickles, giggles or wakes you up to be alive. Are you criticizing yourself every day for doing nothing productive? When you try to share these with your friends or family, do they understand you? If they don't understand you, does that make you feel lonely? Are you lost somewhere? Do you think nobody will understand you? Do you wonder why everything is so complex with you? Does all of these frustrate you? Have you lost the confidence once you had? Have you acquired some bad habits which are bad for your health?

After finishing this book, you will figure out which direction to go in your life. You will find the peace of mind in almost every situation. You will learn to cope up with the fear of failures. You will know that creating your own passion is better than finding it. You will get back your interest in life, and you will learn to experience and live every moment. You will stop criticizing yourself and others for everything in life. You will lose the feeling of being lost and lonely. You will find the hope to be the better you. Everything is going to be simple in your life. You will gain the self-confidence, and you will build new habits to achieve great milestones in your life.

College, final year, the time when companies visit the campus for placements. The whole thing was very new to me, my friends and my batch mates. I and my friends were pretty sure that we would not get pass the interview of the very first company that would visit our college. As we knew, that the company had very high standards for the selection process. They were definitely looking for another Mark Zuckerberg or Bill Gates. Anyway it didn't matter to us as we were confident that we would ace the interview of the next company which was a mass-recruiter (Organization which hires many students at once during college placements). That was like a Mesiah for students like us, you know, average ones. We had hope in it. We got nice formal attires for ourselves. We were all ready to rock and roll. No matter what, that was it, a happy ending. Well, guess what, I and my friends were knocked out in the first round. It came to us as a surprise and a shock. Because we had our future plans which only starts after getting a job in that company. All those trips and wandering all over India, all got shattered, in just a few minutes. Placement head was shocked to see that they hired about 60% of what they hired the pervious year. I was sure that night he couldn't sleep well. He was a very nice guy. That incident was a bit eye opener for all of us. Still, we hoped to get a chance somehow. Time went by, many companies came, and I wasn't getting a job. There were students passing the interviews of very prestigious companies, and I was okay with that because somehow I knew that they deserved it. At the same time, I resented some of them for getting selected who according to me wasn't deserving. But in reality, they all deserved what they got.

As our final year was about to an end, all of the well-known companies had hired from our college and the chances of getting hired in one of the good companies were decreasing. Like anybody, I was broke from within. You know, leaving home for the interview with hope to get a job, and failing at the first round itself. Then, coming back home, and the family asks about what happened at the interview, and I had to say I didn't get selected. With time, I hated that question. I was angry, and I have kept everything inside of me. As I can't shout out on anyone for not getting a job, as it wasn't anyone's fault. It was crushing me. When I chose to do engineering, almost everyone had said to my father that there was no scope in the engineering. I had assured my father to not worry, if I won't get any job then I could open my own business. I could sense that he didn't feel assured with it, and still he supported me with my college. My whole family did support me. After all, I was the first engineer in my family, and I think the first one to complete the graduation.

I was broke as this thought crossed my mind what everyone had said to my father. And I didn't say what I was going through to anyone, as always I like to keep everything to myself. I was scared to death. But there was only one person in my life with whom I have shared my feelings. I have never met her in person. She was a friend from a foreign land, met on the internet, and shared almost every piece of life to her. She supported me and gave me hope to never give up. I think I promised her to keep her in my book if I ever write one. Her name was Celina. It really nice to have someone like that in life. She knew what I was going through.

Time, life, health, mind, friends, family and almost everything, I was losing. My heart and body was crushed under the pressure of having no job. I had lost weight a lot. Haha, and already I was a very skinny guy. It was horrible. I wanted to give up. I had lost myself, my unique qualities and personality. I wanted to work at the place with less formal culture. So I asked myself that is formal attire important for interview? Is company going to hire the people who look good in formals? If it would be my clothes, then I am sure I should have got placed in the first company itself. After thinking a lot, I decided to not wear formals for my next interview. As I took the decision, I felt an urge of freedom within me. One day, a company was about to visit the campus. I haven't heard of it much. I wore what I liked, and I kept myself casual without worries. I told myself if I won't get this, it will be the company's loss and not mine. The result of the first round came as a surprise. I passed the first round, and it was really weird to me. All the students who got filtered for the second round which was a technical interview. They started to rush to get the formals. As no one had expected to be in the second round so no one was wearing formals except a few. One of my friends came to me and asked me about my clothes, I said no man, I am going like this, casually. Damn, that confident, I could win the entire universe with that. In the second round, I went for the technical interview. To my surprise, I passed it too. I would like to give the credit to my clothes, which gave me the confidence to be me. So I was waiting for the third round, which was a managerial round. I passed it as well. After that, I had to wait for 2-3 hours for the result. The hiring process was almost coming to an end. They had already hired more than they planned to hire from our campus. It was the last moments of the hiring process of the company and some of the interviewers started to leave. It is then a voice from the inside was saying that it's done, nothing will happen here too. There were only 6 students left waiting for the results. And HR came out and called one student out of six who were waiting for the result. And other 5 thought that it's done and he got selected. I started to pack my bag to go home with the disappointment. To our amazement, HR told that guy that he could go home, and he was done for the day. I was sad for him and then HR called 5 of us. Told us the surprisingly unbelievable news that we were selected.

Hurray!!! Awesome!! Yuhooooo!!! So that fine day, after getting nearly 22 rejections from the companies, and failing to fulfill the criteria to even sit for the interview of some of the prestigious companies. I finally got the job. I was so happy. Without disclosing this news to anyone, as I wanted to surprise my family first. On my way back home, I bought my favorite sweets and reached home. My mom, brother, and sister were watching television. I took the sweets out of the bag and gave it to my mom telling her that her son got the job. It was priceless to see the glow and happiness in the eyes of my mom, brother and sister.

After one or two years after getting the job, I was happy with my company and the salary I was getting paid, I liked the work culture. I haven't given any thought about what I will do after my college and placement. Some of the students have it already figured out even before entering the college. I didn't do that planning for myself. For some time, I kept on enjoying the perks of being employed. With time, something started to dawn on me, it was making me think about my future. What was I going to do in my life now? Should I keep up with the job? Should I go for higher studies? If yes, then which higher studies? Here at my place or in a foreign land? What If I would fail with this or that? What If I didn't get succeed? With all these questions in mind, I tried to talk to many people including my peers, colleagues, friends, family and my seniors at the office. I read books related to life and its problems. I have watched motivational, inspirational and some knowledgeable videos too.

I kept this for about a year and still couldn't figure out what to do next in life. I have learned many things but couldn't decide what to do next. With the confidence, which was lost this time, and the fear of failure that has dawned on me. I had lost interest in almost everything, and I was like a walking dead. The peace of mind, oh forget it. Even I was doing meditation every day, it wasn't working the way it should. When I was going through all of these, something happened between me and Celina. I lost her due to some unavoidable circumstances. It made me lonely, no one seemed to understand and listen to me. I was lonely without any hope for a better future. It was frustrating and everything in life seemed so complex. About the health, don't ask, it was unexpectedly going bad.

Unconsciously, I did build some habits like getting addicted to my phone, fear of failure, losing, being a walking dead and watching a lot of series without a break. All was going down. Until I have figured out ways to get out of this and getting my life back in my hands just like before during my college days.

I am writing this book to share those ways that I did to get back my life. I have described and summarized everything for you to implement in your life to get control over it. To make sure these will work for you too, just do the required actions. I am going to divide the book into several chapters, and each chapter will work as a milestone in your journey of transformation. I will suggest to read a chapter and let your mind digest it before moving on to the next.

Do each exercise suggested for about a week at least to get the real taste of it. See the wonders happening within you. You will know when you will do it for yourself. I hope and wish you all the best on this journey of life transformation.

Let's relax a bit now.

RELAX

"Rule your mind or it will rule you." ~ Buddha

Only when the dust settles in the glass of water, we can see through clearly. When there is a clear sky, we can see the stars. Only with the clean lens, we can shoot a clear photo. Only when the mind is calm, we can see our life as it is.

Before I begin to tell you about the methods to transform your life. I want you to have a relaxed state of mind. Right now, you might be feeling down, discouraged, threatened, frustrated, hopeless, crushed, and all alone. This section of the book will let you know about some little ways to bring peace to your mind. It will help you to be conscious of yourself. By doing these exercises, you will become aware of your actions, and slowly you will start to live in the moment. These exercises have helped me many times to remove the dust from my mind and helped me to see my life as it is. I hope it will do wonders for you as well. Do the exercise for about a week to make it work for you. With all my best efforts, I will provide the methods which had worked for me tremendously. I believe that quality is much better than quantity.

So let's get started.

Taking a bath with awareness

In Indian culture, which has taught the world to be at ease, believe that taking a bath not only cleans the physical body. It also helps to clear the mind. It brings relaxation all over the body and the mind. It might sound weird to some, but most of you know it. Some of you have already felt it. Nowadays, we have lost the sense of awareness towards our actions. It means that we are not aware of this very moment i.e. now. We are sitting in a meeting room with our mind wandering somewhere else. Listening has become a difficult task as we are so busy with our thoughts a lot. With the lack of awareness towards our actions, we are moving towards a black hole of our lives. We let go of the precious moment of our lives slip away because we are involved with our thoughts all the time. It is not turning out to be something great for us. We have become like walking dead. We are so busy with those little devices in our hands that we are ignoring the most precious things in our lives.

We don't look up and talk to the other person sitting next to us. We look down and time passes like a bullet train. There is a need to bring our awareness to every action we do. To be calm, we need to bring awareness into this moment. At this moment, we are aware of the thoughts going on in our minds. We only need to shift it into another direction. We have to bring a shift in our mindset to become aware of this very moment. With this fast-paced lifestyle and this multitasking culture, it's not easy to be consciously aware of almost everything around us. When being aware of this very moment becomes our second nature. It will be a phenomenal shift in our lives. To give you a start, I want you to practice to bring the concious awareness while you shower.

In the Himalayas, there was a princess, Uma, who wanted to learn yoga to attain the Supreme. Shivendra was a well-known yogi at that time and place. She went out in search of him. He was outside the city, was in his deep meditation. She sat there and thought to wait for him till he comes out of his meditative state. The moment she sat, he opened his eyes and asked the girl for the reasons for being there. She explained her desire to attain the Supreme.

Before accepting any disciple, every guru took a test to know their potential. Shivendra took the test of Uma and accepted her as his disciple. Uma requested him to come to the palace. He told her that she can go, he will be there within the next two days. Her excitement wasn't easy to hide. She was happy after getting accepted by the guru. She went back to her palace. She was waiting for the guru on the day he assured his arrival. She was full of excitement and fear. She wanted to give the best hospitality to the guru. Sun has moved from east to the west. Now, the guru reached the palace. Uma went to arrange for Guruji's food. A separate room was arranged and decorated for the Guruji. Uma was told to start her lessons from the next morning by the Guru.

Next morning, Uma comes to the Guru. Uma offers her pranam, he was sitting on the aasan (a place to sit). Uma said she was excited to know what she will learn under his guidance, and was grateful to her Guru. She was about to touch his feet as a gesture recieve blessings from him, he stopped her in midway and asked her to take a bath & come. But she had already taken the shower. She said before puja she always takes a bath, but was again told to follow his order. Uma looked confused.

Uma came before the Yogi after having a bath. He told her to go and bath again. This continued to happen for another 2-3 times. Uma was infuriated on being asked to bathe again and again. She tried to explain to him that she had taken a lot of baths that day. The Guru told her she will have to keep doing this, to the point that she feels each and every drop of water on her body.

Uma's parents, King and the Queen asked the Guruji what does this lesson means? Shivendra said that in search for materialistic pleasures, we forget the smallest experiences in life - be it even having a bath. When we realize the smallest pleasures - like that of having each drop fall on our body while bathing, it's then that we are awakened from within. Thus by doing this Uma will be ready for her next step. Uma goes near the bathing place and steps into the pond and pours water over her head. And then slowly she herself feels each and every drop on her body, and she begins to glow.

She was ready for the next step.

To learn anything in your life, you need to have a clear mind which will help you to understand and retain the knowledge you learn. So, let's clear your mind with this exercise. Whenever you take a shower, just bring your attention to the flow of water over your body. Feel water droplets flowing down all over. Pay attention to the flow. The sensations it brings in different parts of the body. Your mind may wander. It may bring up thoughts that you never want to face in your life. Thoughts that will distract you from your path of becoming aware. The mind is very smart, it doesn't want you to take control over it. It will do its best to distract you from becoming aware of this moment. Don't worry about all these thoughts. Remember that thoughts are not real and these are only generations of our minds. So, it is okay to get distracted in the beginning. Just be aware of this distraction and bring back your awareness to the flow and each droplets. No need to do it forcefully. Just accept your thoughts as it is and let those thoughts go. It doesn't matter how worse or beautiful those thoughts can be, just let those go.

At the end of the shower before you wipe your body with a towel, just sit or stand, and close your eyes to feel the water droplets flowing down over the body. If you find yourself distracted, just be aware of this distraction and bring back your awareness to the flow of water droplets. And when you will open your eyes, you will feel calm and peaceful.

A shower is an essential activity of our day, and it helps to clean the body and mind. Never hurry while you take a shower. This practice will bring a certain peace to your mind, and you will see your life situation from a different view. Just like when the dust settles in the glass of water, only then you could see through theglass.

Write down your feelings out on the paper

Bring a habit of journaling in your life. Feeling frustrated about something happened in your day. Well, write it out on a piece of paper and throw it away. Try it yourself. Take a pen and paper, start writing whatever comes into your mind without filtering anything. Don't think at all before taking it all out of your mind because no one is going to read it and in the end, you're going to throw it away. This exercise will help you to take all the shit out of your head onto the paper which you can throw away for forever. When a thought is in your head, it lingers there because your mind believes all thoughts it creates are great. And why not? After all, thoughts are the invention of our mind, and for an inventor, its every invention remain great. So, when you write it all out on the piece of paper, it gives a sense to the mind that its invention got the necessary attention. It tells the thought has been worked upon and now the mind may let it go. There is no obligation to keep it in the memory for any longer. Therefore, this is one of the best methods to clean up the mind and bring it to relaxation.

Once upon a time, my best friend has left without telling me any reason except kept on saying that it was not good for us to be in connection for more. She left. We had a pretty profound bond with so little time, like five or six months. We used to talk about everything from our eating habits to the stars and galaxies, from religion to spirituality, and from art to science. We knew about each other a lot. We used to talk a lot. Then something happened, and she had to leave. The reason for that is still unknown. That left me abashed. I had no one else to talk about anything. I was alone. Although I was living with my family and had friends in college, still I was alone. Loneliness has started to dawn over me. I tried to cry at night. I heard somewhere that crying helps to lighten the burden from the shoulders. So I tried it, and crying doesn't come naturally to me. After some days had passed, I woke up early in the morning and I went on the roof. I felt the void she had created in my life. That how this sun was still there, and that wind was there, water, birds, sky, mood, trees, and everything was there, except hers. I had a thought to write everything out. So, I had opened my laptop and visited my blog. It is my personal journal and only selected few can see it. I wrote everything that came to my mind without filtering it out, and my hands were just moving on the very keyboard on which I'm writing this book on. As I kept on writing and writing, I started to feel lighter and lighter, my mind started to get decluttered and it got clean, just like pure water. I could see through. I realized it then that writing can be a stress buster too.

I think that's why many people in this world write in a journal, to get everything out of the mind. To take out all the trash away. Just experiment with this method and see if it works for you or not. Take out a few minutes, let's say ten minutes and a pen and paper or your laptop, and start writing whatever comes into your mind. I can assure after you will finish it for the first time, you will feel different. You will see the life from a different perspective. Now, go and clean up your mind.

Get lost in your world

"Sometimes when you lose your way, you find YOURSELF." ~ Mandy Hale

Everyone has their way to relax. Some of us like to sleep a lot to let the mind clear out on its own by closing all the senses. Some of us like to exhaust themselves till they get tired to the extent that they'll fall asleep as soon as they lie on the bed and it may help them to forget their worries and in turns, gives them relaxation a bit. Some like to watch tv or videos on the internet to relax which I will not recommend as you will only be filling your mind with more data instead of emptying it out.

I would like you to do some things which makes you involve your any of the 5 physical senses such as running, drawing, singing, dancing, cleaning the house, do the dishes, washing, cooking or anything that could help you to get lost with yourself.

Only way to be sure that you are found is to get lost somewhere first. Important aspect of this is to have a distance from your problems and worries for a little while, giving your mind a break from it. Because the other time when you will be seeing towards your problems from a different perspective. It will help you when we will discuss on how to get over a problem in another chapter.

Best way to get lost in our own world is to do what we love to do. And in this time, I know it's hard to understand what you love and what you don't. As you are unable to understand your emotions, except feeling them low most of the time throughout the day.

ou can start with whatever you used to do when you were a child that made you happy. For example, I like to draw and sketch, so I made a deal with myself that whenever I would feel that things are getting so stressful, I will remind myself to sketch on a sticky note and stick it on my desk wall. It helps to keep my desk creative and my mind clean. I also like to make things out of paper and the world knows this art with the name of origami. I had a dragon on my desk and it was so cool, everyone who came onto my desk loved it. Unfortunately, someone stole it. Anyway, the point is that I get lost in my own world when I do anything like that. Especially when I create something.

Creating things is in the DNA of all of us, and we all want something that we built for ourselves.

It is one of the things I do that helps me to take a few things out of my mind and make some space there for other things to work on. Whenever I feel overwhelmed of everything around me, I start to empty my mind. Be it cleaning the room, or organizing my cupboard, or maybe creating some arts, writing something, whatever seems feasible for me to do, I do it to create some space and give my mind a break.

So why wait, you may get lost in your own world, and if you don't have one, then make one.

How can we bring our mind to the state of peace?

Till now, we have looked towards some ways to bring relaxation in our lives. We learned to realize the smallest pleasures – like that of feeling each drop fall on our body. We learned to pass our thoughts on the paper which helps to clear the mind. We learned to get lost in our own world to give ourselves the refreshment our mind need.

Purpose of this chapter is to bring you on the state of relaxation so that your mind could become more focused on the important aspects of you and your life. I recommend to relax first by practicing these exercises or any of these would do, and read a chapter, give yourself time to digest and implement the methods explained in each of them, then move on to the next one. Or find your own pace of going forward from now onwards, go fast forward, go slow, flip pages from begin to end or end to start, it's your choice. As long as you do the exercises, it shall work for you.

Just remember that the book will work for you when you will work for yourself.

ACCEPTING YOUR KARMA

"The quality of your life is entirely your making and nobody else and nobody else." ~ Sadhguru

Karma is in fashion these days. Lots of talks are going on karma. In India, karma is given a special value in one's life. We come across people telling us that whatever is happening to us is the result of our karma, whatever it may be, good or bad, anything. We can say karma is like an echo in the mountain, whatever it may sound, it comes back to us. It is a common belief that good karma results in good things and bad karma results in bad things.

"What you sow is what you reap." ~Unknown

What is karma? If anyone tells us about our karma's consequences in our life, have we ever asked the person that what the hell is karma? How may we define it? Even if we have asked it, what kind of answers did we get? We might have got the answers that karma is what we do in our life, how we treat others, how we live, how we go on in our lives and so on.

In simple words, karma means action. Whether you do it through your body, mind, or emotion. Whatever you do or however you do, it stores that in you karmic baggage. Now what is karmic baggage? It is the place which keeps the record of all the karma you are building up. It is like a memory imprint, and it's all within you. Now whatever decision you will take today maybe influenced from something you did years ago.

Let's take a simple example, you went out for a walk in the cold weather wearing all the winter clothes, but you didn't feel the need to wear a cap and a scarf. Next day, you get cold, and you start to blame something or someone for your sickness. Now tell me, isn't this the result of your own karma? If you would have gone out with a cap and a scarf as well, had you been got this cold? Might be yes or no. It also depends on your immune system. And if your immune system is weak, you might start to blame your immune system for not keeping you healthy. Is your immune system weak by itself or is it your doing that made it weak? Do a retrospection yourself.

At the moment you might be agitated, distressed, lost, wounded, hopeless, guilty, fatigued and/or anything. I ask you to take some deep breaths right now.

Please do this as you read. Keep your spine straight, not too tight, just in a relaxed way, inhale gently through your nose and gently exhale it fully through your mouth. Keep inhalation and exhalation for upto 3-4 seconds each. If possible please close your eyes as well. Do this for 5-6 times, and you can do it more if you wish. Do it now before moving to the next paragraph.

Did you finish the deep breathing? I'm counting on you on this.

Now I want you to analyze your life a bit. Take any one of the problems you are encountering or the one you have faced in the past. You need to think about how the obstacle came into your life. Through which door it has entered. Do not blame others. Don't say that it has happened or is happening in your life because of a particular person or a specific situation has arisen.

Examine it like Sherlock Holmes. See all the evidence before coming to any conclusion. See it through every perspective. I want you to analyze it and look for your actions that allowed it to enter in your life. You may also think about how you have reached this peak of your career or life. Recall about all the decisions you have made so far to come here, maybe those decisions were taken by you consciously or subconsciously. Might be possible that you took those decisions under the influence of your elders or due to peer pressure. Whatever may be the reasons behind those choices you have taken so far. Now imagine how different your life would be if you would have done things differently.

You would realize that wherever you are right now, be it at the depth of your own hell or at the top of your own heaven, whether you are success or failure right now. You would be able to see that you are here because of the decisions you took in the past. No one did the hard work that you did to make yourself a success or no one did the lazy or senseless work that you did to make yourself a failure.

Let's think about the way you are right now. You may have a broken heart from one relationship, and that is still effecting you. As if your trust was broken then you would not want to trust anyone else again for the same thing. Or even if you decide to enter another relationship with someone else, then naturally you would be taking all the precautions to save your trust from getting broken again. Why naturally? Have you ever noticed it when people say that it is natural to be afraid after first heartbreak? Why is it so? Because the karma you have built up using your body, mind and emotion, now it is stored and influencing your present decisions. In fact, it is influencing the very personality you carry today. I hope it showed you how the karma works in the bigger picture. If we have to see how it works at a smaller level, let's see a simple example. To pass the exam, you will study or cheat. If you won't get caught cheating during the exam and get enough marks to pass, you pass the exam otherwise you get failed. It all ends up with the results of all the actions you performed.

Even if you do not understand the nature of karma, don't worry. Just know that the way of your life is entirely your doing and no one else's.

Now you might say that yeah everything is your doing in your life but the person shouldn't have done this with me or a particular event shouldn't have happened in a certain way. Stop this nonsense. Stop blaming others for the kind of life you are living. You are the creator of your life, either you will create a masterpiece or trash, depends on you.

When you realize that your life is entirely your making, then it gives you the power to change the way you want it to be. Once you realize that whatever is happening in your life, the experience you are generating within, is entirely your making and nobody else's. It gives the control to change your life in your hands.

Now, you will stop blaming others for your situations. You are doing certain kind of actions in your life which are resulting in the quality of your life right at this moment.

Why didn't I merge this chapter into some other ones? Because I want you to know that this is important, and it requires our special care. When you change your perception about your life, karma, and its results. It gives you the mindset to do something about your problems. When you realize that this is all because of your actions only, then and then only you can work something out to solve the problem. Then and only then you will be ready to take the responsibility for your own life. Otherwise, you will keep on blaming others, and in this way, subconsciously you will be giving the control of your life in the hands of others. Be careful about that, a few are there to make your life better, not everyone.

Here is an exercise that I want you to do to get the control of your life in your hands.

Remind yourself that "The quality of my life is entirely my making and nobody else and nobody else."

Do it in the morning when you wake and at night when you are about to go to sleep. You can remind yourself this at any time of the day. Let this thought dawn over your mind. Let yourself be aware of this. Experiment with it for at least a week or so before moving forward in this book.

I would like to tell you that this sentence has changed the way I used to approach my problems. Whenever I am stuck in a problem, or I find myself blaming others. I take a few deep breaths and remind myself that the quality of my life is entirely my making and nobody else and nobody else.

Accepting our results of our actions gives us the freedom to bring the remarkable changes in our lives.

Now, I want you to relax and take control of your life at this very moment.

Just remember, you're the creator of your own life and nobody else and nobody else.

PROBLEM

It sucks to get stuck in one place for a long time. Do you feel like you have hit the wall? Not literally, but you can't see anything ahead. Do you have various paths which may lead to different places? Are you confused about which way to go to? Does it scare you to be stuck here for you entire lifetime? Or ending up at the wrong place scares you the most? Which fear do you fear the most? What is holding you back? You have a lot of options, and you can't figure out which one to choose, because you are scared that it may lead to something dangerous. Does any of these sound like you? Then read on.

Why are you afraid now? You have brave till this moment. What is it that causing this fear within you? I understand you very well. As I was in the same hole. It may be hard for me to know what you are going through at this moment, and I think that you can get out of this pit as well. I think that if you can make this far in your life, then you can surely go through this one too.

I was going through the same confusion in my life about what to do next. I didn't want to limit myself to one place, and yes, I wanted a good salary. I wanted to expose myself to new places. I wanted to work in a foreign land. I have had some choices to choose from, such as study abroad or here in India, or go for a management study or technical one, and possibly decide to switch my employer to the one who will have challenging work, and will pay me more.

The early twenties is a very complicated stage for anyone. It is a transition phase from being a teenager to an adult. To become responsible about our own life, be self-dependent on most our expenses, have a job with plans for future, at the same time explore the world and don't forget to look after our elders as well.

I didn't know what it is? Why it is? I had no idea. Lots of things to do at this age. I have tried asking lot of my seniors, colleagues, peers, collegemates, friends, family and basically, whoever I met. It was a mess.

Do you want to know how I knocked out many of my options? I started to write. I wrote out everything on a piece of paper, well you can say papers, as I have written a lot regarding my choices.

One day, what I did was that I took a notebook and a pen, wrote a title on the top of the page "Study abroad (MS)," and I have written about the lifestyle that I might get if I choose this option for my future.

- I asked myself whether studying abroad would benefit me in any way besides getting a job abroad.
- What will it cost me in time and money?
- Is there any other way I can enjoy the same benefits as after doing MS (getting a job abroad)?
- Is it worth to do MS?

After answering these questions to myself, I have got my answer. Then I decided to not to go to study abroad.

As I had finalized my choice, I got a news from my friend that he is going to study abroad the next month. And it created a doubt in my choice. I thought that maybe I should rethink my decision. As it was about to move me from the resolution I made the day before. I reminded myself that I had made my choice after thinking a lot, and I have trust in myself that I can't be wrong in this.

I see a path that he doesn't see. Moments which will throw me away from the choice I have taken had started to come into my life, again and again, and was making me to doubt my decision. But I kept my ground. As Steve Jobs said that focus isn't only about saying yes to one thing, but it also about saying no to trillion things that come your way.

When all was fine, I got to hear about another friend who is also planning to go to study abroad. And I was like she told me that she might go to study abroad. But then she has changed her decision. Guess what I still kept my resolution because what I am seeing, no one is seeing that. Sometimes it becomes hard to believe ourselves, but it's worth to believe in ourselves, no matter what.

Now when I see back, I don't even remember about why I took that decision. One thing I can say to myself that I did take the best decision as per that moment. And there is no need to put my intelligence at work for the same thing again and again. I am happy with my choice.

Let me share with you about how to deal with a problem in your life. No matter what kind of problem it is. Or how big it seems. The technique that I have used to solve my problems. **Writing** .

Start by asking yourself a few questions, and when you will reach the last question, your problem would be solved. Don't be shocked, it is the power of writing, which lets the problem solver to come out of our mind.

What is the root cause of the problem?

To understand the reason to ask this question, let's hear my stupid story about how I discover kidney stones.

You know sometimes, the source of the disease is something else, and we feel pain somewhere else. For example, a few months back I started to feel nausea after eating anything during any time of the day, I thought it is related to my digestive system, and my doctor thought this too. After getting the medicines, I felt alright, and after some time(a few weeks), the same symptoms started to happen again. I got the antibiotics from the doctor again, and it worked, I felt amazingly fine.

One day, relatives were there at home, my mom discussed my symptoms with them, you know, how family talks can be. So my aunt suggested me to have an ultrasound of my whole abdomen. Same symptoms occurred again, this time I went for the ultrasound of my entire stomach, and I was shocked to find out that I have stones in my left kidney. Then on the internet, when I started to search about this, I found that nausea feeling is one of the symptoms of kidney stones. By the way, it's not good to rely on the internet for our medical diagnosis.

I understood that my body was giving me signs, and I couldn't understand it.

So yeah, take a few deep breathes and then think and then start writing about the root cause of the problem.

What can you do about it?

Write about all the solutions that you can come up with. Write about the consequences of each and every solution that you might choose to do to solve this particular problem.

For example, in my case I figured what food I could eat or what I couldn't and list goes long.

What is the best solution?

Choose one that suits you the best. Take the decision that you are going to implement to solve the problem. For example, in my case I could go for a treatment with medicines or have the surgery. And I decided to go with the former.

Take action over it.

Now you have done all the theory work till here, and it is time to bring it in practice. It is time to take action. Yeah... bingo... go for it.

You can experiment with your decision as well to see which fits well for you. Life is an experiment, so live it the way you want to live and not just the fairytale one.

Now try these steps right now, take a pen, a notebook and take a problem to knock it out of your life. Ask yourself following questions and write answers

- What is the root cause of this problem?

- What can you do about it?
- What is the best solution?
- Take action over it.

Till now, you've learned to relax, took control of your life in your hands and acquired problem-solving skills. Now, let's move on to fight the fear of failures.

FEAR OF FAILURES

"Do your duty without worrying about its fruit." ~ Srimad
Bhagvad Geeta

When we sense danger or a threat from anyone or anything, it ignites fear in us. Failure, of course, can be a threat to our lives or it can be a stepping stone towards a better life. It depends on our response towards the failure. It is simple, isn't it?

What if I fail? What if I do not succeed at what I will decide? What if I get success in the beginning and get a failure at the end of it? What if I get success and don't feel successful? What if it doesn't work? What if I choose the wrong path? What if I take a wrong decision? What if I don't find my passion? What if it is not for me? If it doesn't work for him then how can I be sure it will work for me? If it is working for him then how can I be so sure that it will also work for me? What if I come last? What if it doesn't make me happy? What if it's not my calling or not my passion? What if I keep on failing at every turn?

Maybe these are a few questions which are wandering inside your mind for so long. Since the moment you have a thought to do something in your life. The moment you had thought to improve yourself, these all self-doubt must have been started to dawn in your awareness. I bluntly want to tell you that I do not have any answers to these questions. These sorts of questions occur in the kind of mind which wants to play safe, without risking anything. Maybe a kind of mind which has gone through some failures recently.

What we don't understand, might also ignite fear in us. When we don't have the surety of something, may also ignite fear in us. For example, we go to our college or office every day by the same route, we know it is okay, and we know we are safe. On another day, if the driver chooses another route, our senses alert us, and we become attentive, trying to absorb as much as we can and understand whether this new route is safe for us and is in the right direction as well.

If you want to experiment with it, then try it with yourself. Choose any fine day of the week, and find a new route to go to your place, you'll find yourself more alert as compared to the general route you used every day. It will fill you with enjoyment, accomplishment, full of confidence and excitement.

Understand this and let it settles within you, if someone else takes you to the new route, your brain will alert you due to the danger that might arise, but when you'll use the new route by yourself, it will fill you with lots of positive emotions.

Failure is the opposite of success. A failure happens when we don't succeed. When we fail in doing something, that's a failure. That's real. In fact, failure helps us to succeed. When we have a fear of failure, that's hypothetical most of the time. When we fear from trying new things in life because of fear of failure, that can be called a failure to live.

We get stuck in analysis-paralysis, in which we keep on analyzing that we are scared when it comes to implementation. We waste a lot of time in just analyzing to know if we would get a success in this path or not. And this way, we don't do anything, we don't achieve anything in life. It's not good.

We need to understand that failure is just a failure, and not the end of our lives. Fearing the fear of failure is a total waste of time and energy. We might waste a lot of energy to find the solutions to not fail at something before even starting it.

When a mountaineer plans the climb on a mountain. She doesn't stick to the plan. She knows that her plan might fail at some point in time during her climb, and at that time she doesn't come back to the foot of the mountain. Instead, she reroute her climb to pass the blockages about which she was unaware at the time she planned her climb. By doing so, she reaches the peak. By accepting her failures on every blockage during the climb, instead of criticizing the nature or mountains. She accepted her responsibilities and changed the route to reach the peak. Imagine, if she would be afraid of unexpected blockages on the climb, and got stuck in what if, what if and what if questionnaire, and wouldn't have started the climb, would she be able to reach the peak ever? No, never, if she hadn't kept the fear of failure aside, she wouldn't have reached the peak of the mountain, and she would have been stuck with the analysis- paralysis.

When I was in the college, I had friends who were really good at clicking photos. Whether it's a DSLR camera or a smartphone, they knew the right angle to click a photo with the right composition. And they also made weird poses while taking a photo, just like any photographer would do to get the perfect angle to capture the moment in the best possible way. When I used to click their photos, they almost all the time criticized my photography skills. I was a self-confident person. And it had hurt my ego. That how dare they would say about my skills. They were telling me the truth. But Iwasn't ready to accept it.

I was browsing the internet and found out about the concept of 30 days of challenge. It was a wonderful idea to develop my skills, and I only had to be committed for anything for 30 days only. Someday, when I was sitting alone on the college ground in the morning, and no one was there. The idea to take 30 days of photography challenge dawn on me. It dawned, but I didn't implement because I was afraid to fail at it. That what would happen if I wouldn't be able to complete this challenge? What would I do if I won't find something new to click the photo of? Would I be able to click the photos in public areas, as I was kind of a shy person?

One day when I was coming back from my college then I had decided to click the photo of anything to get it started. Fear was there. Questions like what would other people will think about me? What if someone just came to me and tell me to not click photos? What if someone laughs at me? What if someone would think of me as a weirdo or an insane?

I was walking with all these fears rising in my mind. That day I decided to not take the rickshaw to my home from the metro station. I came out of the station, started to walk towards my home. I saw the construction of the new metro line on the way just a minute walking distance. I was afraid of all those questions and fears. I took the photo while walking. I didn't dare to stop even for a minute. I just stood there for like one or two seconds and clicked the button, and a photo was clicked. I was good to go.

I was terrified before taking the shot, but after accomplishing this task, I felt so relieved and my heart was filled with excitement. That was the moment of my first winning over the fear. I felt so amazing afterward. I did some editing and uploaded it to show my friends that I had started this journey of 30 days of photography challenge. The best part about this was, I decide the rules. I kept the rules simple i.e. click a photo a day for the next 30 days, no photos should be the same and upload it on the social network. I had asked of my friends to join me in the journey. Some had joined and started the same day or after a while.

When I started this challenge, I didn't know, and I wasn't sure that I will finish it successfully. I was scared, especially to take photos in the public places like metro stations, bus stands, or the places where it is not common to take photos. I was terrified when I had started the challenge. But somehow, after taking the first photo, I got some self-confident and excitement to do it more. I learned many new things about photography which I would have never learned if I had never started this challenge.

One important thing I learned that we don't actually need a DSLR camera to click nice photos. Photography skills are a must for taking mesmerizing photos. Even DSLR camera won't be able to make the photos look good if you don't have enough skills to handle it.

◆ ◆ ◆

Observe yourself carefully, and you will find out that you don't like fears in your life.

Ask yourself why do you think/want to do things that might create fear in you? If you had ever won over your fear in your life, which I can be sure of that you had won over your fear many times in your life. Because that is the reason, you are here at the moment reading this book. Somehow you have lost the confidence in you to win over your fears.

Our mind likes challenges. You give a challenge to yourself, and if the challenge is tempting enough, then you will find your body and mind working together to win that challenge. Otherwise, your body and mind might create friction within yourself. For example, at night, your eyes are heavy, feeling like someone has put tons of weight over your eyelids. And your mind doesn't care because your mind is busy in stalking your crush, scrolling the newsfeed, texting with many people in different apps, and maybe you're also on call with your loved ones at the same time. Mind is busy with multitasking and body is telling you that it needs rest and a moment come, when the person on call keeps on talking and you went into sleep, your friends and family on various texting apps are getting angry over you because you have left them in seen, and while sleeping you had sent a friend request to your crush without even realizing it. And you already know what happens in the morning afterward.

Whenever fear starts to enter in your mind, try to know if its real or not. For example, if fear arises because you're thinking to go in front of the lion, then it's totally real fear as it's life threatening to you. But if you think to do an activity, and that's not a crime, and still fear arises in you, then question the fear.

Ask yourself these questions at the time of fear

- What is the worst that could happen?
- Is it really worse? (Because our minds like to exaggerate things)

Once you will answer these questions your fear will vanish, and you will get the confidence to do the thing you were thinking for a long time to do.

Even if it doesn't work, then remind yourself that you are a mortal being. Say to yourself this lovely question that Steve Jobs asked himself every day.

"If today were the last day of my life. Would I want to do what I am about to do today?"

Sooner, you will know if it is worth doing or not. When you'll know about its worth, then no fear will work in front of the fear of death.

Everyone afraid of death. Every fear seems so little in front of death. I'm sure you will do what you want to do and will win over your fears.

If nothing works, then just do it anyway for fun.

Believe me, it's be a great fun or a great story to tell.

WASTING TIME

We are wasting a lot of time these days and at the end of the day, we criticize ourselves for not being productive and not finishing anything that we had decided in the morning. It has become like our ritual to not do anything much and criticize ourselves at the end of the day. If we look closely at it, then it has become one of our habits.

No matter wherever I go and talk to people, most of them have the same thing to say to me that they have done nothing today or yesterday or on the weekend and the time slipped away from their hands. It's kind of habitual now and dangerously becoming a very common thing among our society. And this is one of the common topics that we talk about in our twenties with almost anyone we meet.

At some point in our conversations, we start talking about it. Amazingly, another person has the solution for this and at the same time, going through the same situation in his own life.

Personally, I don't like to listen to these people who are ready to give unused advices to others. People are going through the same situation, and they haven't applied it on themselves but are ready to teach the world.

Let's dive into the ways we're wasting our time.

What is wasting of time?

Let's understand what actually a waste of time is. What does it really mean? Is even talking to our friends also a waste of time? Is spending time with family also a waste of time? Is watching TV really a waste of time? Or maybe spending time scrolling the feeds on any social media platform a waste of time? Or maybe walking to home from a nearby metro station instead of taking a ride is a waste of time as well? Maybe giving time to our hobbies is a waste of time? Or going into details of any subjects when those details are not much important for the exam or to the world, is a waste of time? Or just sitting in front of a computer, bored and browsing anything to find anything that might interest you is a waste of time? Or using your phone instead of talking to the person sitting next to you is a waste of time? I'm sure some questions might also have arisen in your head. So what exactly is a waste of time?

We have tons of things to do, and yet we still find ourselves saying to each other that we've wasted our time. Ask yourself, have you ever tried to understand what exactly is a waste of time? Have you actually tried to define it for yourself? Think about it.

According to my life's experience, "Anything that doesn't have meaning and importance for a person, and the person gives time to that activity or anyone, the spent time is equivalent to a waste of time for that person." Things which does not add value in your life as compared to the other things which have importance as well as meaning in your life. Having a different kind of experience is also adding some value in your life.

And when you choose to do things which are of less importance for you, then at the end of the day you will feel like you've wasted time because you could have given that time to the things that actually matter to you. That's the reason there's a technique called **prioritizing** used to spend your time of the day on the things that matter you most.

Now let's see the ways we waste our time, not every way applies to you, but there's no harm in knowing the other possible ways to waste your time, I mean to have some varieties...

- **Senseless arguments:-** Arguments which doesn't have any sense at all are known as senseless arguments. Pardon me with the silly definition of the issue, just know, I'm an engineer. Continuing by giving the examples of senseless arguments such as arguing over veg vs non-veg, god's existence vs non-existence, arguing with your loved ones for forgetting your birthday or anniversary.

- **Social Media:-** As a human being, Facebook is one of the best creation ever created until now. We know the number of people is connected with each other, no matter the distance between them, has found their lost relatives through Facebook, it's easy to find a like-minded person on social media. There are a lot of protests that have gained popularity through social media, and many people have helped others in need. All of these and many other things that may require to write another book on it to get into details have been done using social media and it's incredible when we see it like this. Unfortunately, many people have started to see it as the tool that waste times, gives you the false feeling of having a lot of friends, and that gives stress, tension, and depression as well. Many people are abusing social media by creating a lot of fake accounts just to spy on other people. Most of us just keep on scrolling through their news feeds, and bang!!! half an hour has vanished away. It's a great tool, and at the same time, it is a great tool to connect with anyone anytime, to get an update about events nearby that you might be interested in, and it's only great when used in limits. Even the water which is the source of life on this planet earth can harm us if taken in high quantity or taken with an excess of alcohol.

- **Television:-** Television is also one of the great inventions that came out of the human mind. Many people say that it is an " **idiot box** ." If you also think so, then I challenge you to build something that can make people addicted to your creation. The whole world is poured out into your home through the TV. Now with internet enabled TV, you can just see anything anytime you want. If your job is to look at the TV and you're getting well paid for it, then it's worth watching TV all day and night. If you're getting anything for free or more than you've paid for, then it's just you're the one who is on sale, and not vice-versa. You're not the customer, you're the product and someone else is the customer to buy you and your attention.

- **Gossiping:-** In this way, we're giving importance to the people who are not important to us, and we're wasting our time talking about them. Complaining about the behavior or saying bad or blaming a specific person. If you don't get it, then observe this one thing that "we never gossip about the people we truly care and love." Why? Ask yourself.

- **Unimportant phone calls:-** Sometimes happen that we are in a middle of doing some important piece of work and the phone ring. When we pick the call, then on the other side is the person who is free and has nothing to do in his free time, so he called you to pass his time. But as you're in middle of some important work, maybe important than the talks of the person on the phone. You know this fact, and still you chose to keep on listening the phone, and that's how you waste your time on unimportant phone calls.

- **TV series:-** Watching a season of a TV series in one go or trying to finish it as soon as possible. It is a total waste of time and at the same time, it drains the energy of your mind and make it lazy. It also unable your mind to absorb the information of an hour or so long episode, and hence you can't understand the series well, the way the creators of the series wants you to get it.

- **Sleeping:-** Yes, sleeping. As we have discussed earlier that anything above the limits is harmful for us. Too much sleeping is also harmful for our physical and mental health. As you've observed that we tend to get more sleep when we're sick because our brain knows that the body needs to rest to recover faster. According to this, no matter how much hour of sleep you're getting in night, if you still feeling sleepy all day then there must be a problem with your body. You need to diagnose the problem. If you're getting 8 hours of sleep in a day, that means you're spending 1/3rd of your day in sleeping. And when you add more hour of sleeping to this by sleeping more number of hours during day, you can calculate this yourself that how much precious amount of time you're wasting in just sleeping, even when you're not sick.

- **Shopping:-** There are lot of people who waste a lot of time in shopping. They go to shopping mall for buying a pillow and end up buying a t-shirts for themselves. It's just an example and you can have an idea yourself, that how much time you spend on this. Self- analysis.

There are some more ways that lead to wasting of time. If you like anything from the list above, you may try the new way to waste your time.

TIME AND MORTALITY

"It's really clear that the most precious resource we all have
is time." ~ Steve Jobs

Time is of great significance for all of us. When someone asks
us to do something, we tend to say that we don't have time.
When we want to include exercise or yoga in our lifestyle but
fail to do so, we say we don't have time. Time seems to fly
fast when we are comfortable, having entertainment,
enjoying the moment and of course, when we are getting
late. When we are sad, bored, have nothing to do and no
internet in our phones, time seems to pass at a snail's pace.

We measure time in years, months, weeks, days, hours,
minutes and seconds. We are measuring our lives with these
units of time. Yet we hardly understand the true nature of

time. We are keeping records of our life with these units. No matter where you look, you'll find the time.

When we were born on this planet, that day we joined the journey of the earth revolving around the sun. When we complete our respective journey around the sun, we call it our birthday. No one knows the number of journeys left in their respective lives. No one can know this. Not to the best of my knowledge.

I have always had a thing about time. I got interested in Steve Jobs' life after reading his quotes regarding time. I didn't know anything about him before he passed away. Sad for me. I read in the newspaper about him and there were some of his quotes.

One of them was

"Your time is limited. So don't waste it living someone else's life." ~ Steve Jobs

It kind of hit me. And I started to read about him, listened to his motivational speech which was very inspiring. I got inspired by his work and the way he lived his life at extremes. There is one thing he tells in his speech which was that " **If you live each day as if it was your last, someday you'll most certainly be right.** " And from that time on he kept asking himself a question every morning while looking into the mirror, " **If today were the last day of my life,**

would I want to do what I am about to do today? " And whenever the answer has been "no" for too many days in a row, he knew he needed to change something.

This one hit me more. During my college, I have tried this method of asking this question to myself every morning, and every time I got "no" or "I don't know" as an answer. There is one thing I noticed that to answer this question I need to have a plan for my day ready. I didn't know exactly what I had to do in a day except going to the college.

As I was unable to plan my day, seeing this hurdle on the way, I thought to use it differently as a reminder to my mortality. So, I started to ask this question to myself whenever I found myself to not step up only because I was scared to get out of my comfort zone.

Whenever I wanted to participate in an event, and I felt scared to register for it because I had never done that. When I had a doubt in a class, and was afraid to ask a question to the professor. Whenever I needed to decide whether to go out and explore the place or stay at home. Whenever I was stuck between my fear and my wants, I asked this question, and it worked like charm.

It removed all the fears and cleared the way for what to do next. Whether it's worth going after this or not. And at that time, I was living my life to the fullest. Asking this question, let us realize our mortality.

When I found my crush in college, I wanted to talk to her and fear kept me back. I asked this question myself and bang!!! I went to her to talk, although I freeze in front of her, the point is I started and won over my fear.

And that's why I became a fan of Steve Jobs because he and I had a common thinking about time and our mortal nature.

To bring the phenomenal changes in our life, we need to understand the great significance of time and our mortality. At the moment, we think that we are immortal, and there's a surety that we will live on for eternity. So we keep on putting things on tomorrow. This is what we call procrastination. Lack of realization of our mortal nature is the key source to procrastination. Think if you might not be available tomorrow to finish what you had pushed on tomorrow, what would you do?

You will soon realize the things that matter to you the most. Be it anything that you were thinking to do for a long time. Maybe you have been thinking to show the gratitude and your love towards your parents. You want to talk to your old friend but couldn't do it because it might be weird. You have always wanted to learn guitar but now you think you don't have time for it. Maybe you were thinking to bring smiles to the face of your loved ones or a stranger but you find it hard. You wanted to learn to drive a car or fly a plane.

When you will realize your mortality, everything will get clear, you will get plenty of time to do whatever really matters to you.

Sometimes I tell myself that I have only a month to live, and then I live that month with a constant reminder of my mortality. I always do more and achieve more in months of my mortal reminders.

As we know that once a moment has passed away then it is impossible to bring it back. We can't go back to the past and live the moment again. For now, the time machine is just a science fiction and nothing more. Most of the time we think to change the past to make it more memorable or to do it the right way.

We should realize that we cannot change the past, and we cannot see the future. With that we don't know when or how we are going to die, we don't know when we are going to run out of breath, we have no way of knowing our time and place of death. It is not about searching for the ways to know about it. It is to realize that time is always keep on going at the same speed. We need to decide how we spend our time here in this universe.

"Speed of time is so subtle that to understand it, years and centuries are not enough."

To ask the question that Steve Jobs had asked himself every day. It might require us to have a pre-planned day. There is an exercise I am doing before I go to sleep. I remind myself that this might be the last night I sleep here, I don't know if I would wake up tomorrow morning or not, this might be my deathbed. Although with all the tiredness of my day without having any energy to involve my brain to think this much. I try my best to remind my mortal nature. When I wake up the next morning, I smile to see that I am still alive. When I see my family and loved ones are also alive, I smile even wider.

To sleep peacefully, I also remind myself that all the burdens, all the relationships and all the responsibilities that I have been carrying over my shoulder whole day are the things that I have acquired during a certain time. I can keep it off and just sleep. I sleep peacefully without any worries. I got inspired to try these exercises by a smart guy named Sadhguru. I found his pieces of advice very useful.

When a person is diagnosed with any disease that could cause her death within some time. The person realizes her mortal nature. And all of a sudden, people like her start to make the most of their lives. If we observe closely, we are in the same boat as well. The only difference is that they're told they have a certain amount of lifespan left in their bucket. Nobody has ever reminded us of our mortal nature. Well, I remind you that you're mortal creature just like anybody else on this planet. It doesn't mean that you'll do anything, only because you might be dead the other day. Don't do that stupidity. Don't do anything that could harm anyone around you. Know this, if you're born then sooner or later your time will be over here.

Think of it as a reminder for your mind, so that it could help you to make the big decision. To clear out all the fear and expectations of others. You can choose what is most important to you. Knowing your mortal reality will keep your mind from making fanciful and irrelevant demands.

Asking ourselves the question that Steve Jobs asked himself for many years every morning while looking in the mirror. Try to experiment with it. Ask yourself this question whenever you find yourself stuck in the mud, or you feel scared from doing anything that you want to do, or you don't see anything ahead like you just hit the wall, or you got your heartbroken or anything that you think is wasting your time. This question will surely help you to know the worth of anything or anyone in your life. Always remember that your time is limited, you're a mortal creature, and everything around will pass someday without giving you an advanced notice.

Just a small reminder every day will help to make your life meaningful. Just like you always want to have.

PASSION

"Follow your passion, be prepared to work hard and sacrifice, and, above all, don't let anyone limit your dreams." ~Donovan Bailey

There has been a lot of talking on "following the passion". Success will follow us only when we will pursue our passion. I am not stating this. It is the hot advice going on in the market. Now people like me, who don't have any passion, what should they do? If you are reading this, I am sure you don't have any passion as well. I welcome you to this family of misfits, possibly, this is a small one.

I have seen motivational speeches, and most of those talk about having a passion. I'm sure you would have done the same as well. You know, everyone is talking about following your passion, whatever it is, but no one has made an effort to define what the hell this passion is. So the time has passed by, and I continued looking my passion here and there, without truly understanding what the passion is in the first place.

Why is it needed? Can't I live without a passion in my life? Why is it not okay to not knowing my passion in life? Why I get the strange stare when people ask me about my passion, and I say I don't know? Why can life become boring without a passion? Why can't I figure out my passion? Why everyone around me has it figured out? Is there any problem with me? What's wrong with me? Won't I ever be successful without a passion? Why am I taking too long to find it?

Before I had started to write this book I didn't know my passion, and even while writing this chapter, yet I don't know my passion. Wow!! Did you just notice my confidence? I don't know my passion, and still, I am writing a chapter on the passion. Observe this level of confidence very carefully. You might think that I am not qualified enough to write about passion as I don't have any. Well, you might want to keep on reading to know the secret of this confidence.

Before we continue our journey on the path of the passion, there is something everyone should learn. Always be confident in what you do. When you are confident in whatever you do, people will follow you and will look up to you. Never let your confidence down. Fake it till you make it.

Once you learn to pretend that you are confident, sooner you will start to feel it.

When I go out with my friends, and we are visiting a new place. Sometimes none of us is familiar with the place. Seeing their baffled faces, and everyone starts to look at one another. I get the feeling that there is a need for a leader. I tell them to follow me, I know where to go. In reality, most of the times I don't know and luckily many times I turned out to be right. To my surprise, they follow me without a doubt. That feeling is so amazing. Even if I know that we are lost, I don't lose the confidence. So, it is true, "fake it till you make it" works for the confidence.

Although, better to have clarity first then there won't be any need of fake confidence. Always prioritize clarity over confidence.

Now let's go back to our passion thing. And remember, it's not possible to fake a passion. Let's see this word "passion" carefully. Be aware, it is dangerous, and it has given many people sleeplessnights.

"Passion is a feeling of intense enthusiasm towards or compelling desire for someone or something." ~Wikipedia.

"Strong and barely controllable emotion." ~Dictionary

Have you seen people talking about politics during elections, at times, they can get uncontrollable while sharing their political opinions. Even if they don't have anything to do with the politics, but they met in a metro or bus for the first time, elections are in the air, they start talking about it, and you can feel their strong and barely controllable emotions when they are having the conversations.

If we go by the description in the dictionary, tell me, are those people passionate about politics, or they need something to talk about during their monotonous journey to home or office? If we go by what Wikipedia says, I don't think if any one of them has any enthusiasm or compelling desire towards any politician. If you had joined their conversations, then you may know that how strong and intense emotions they have about their political opinions.

Recently, before I had started to write this chapter I have asked a few of my friends, and colleagues about whether the passion is necessary to live the life? A friend told me that yes passion is necessary to live the life, because, without passion, life is monotonous, similar to a zombie. I was like okay, wasn't satisfied with his answer. And I had another question in my pocket waiting to come out at the right moment like this. I asked him if he has any passion and to this, he replied no, he doesn't have any passion right now. I was like okay, and then he started to explain the reasons for why he doesn't have a passion at the moment.

Another one told me that passion isn't needed to live a life, but then the life would be limited, dull, comfortable, and plainly as it is, life will merely pass by with time. I was feeling nice after hearing this because I have got a surety that I could live my life without a passion. Wow!!! That is amazing. Again I have fired my next question asking about if he has any passion, the answer was no. I felt that his answer was somehow acceptable.

Here comes my another friend, and she talks much better than her looks. When you see her, you may see her as an intellectual being, but she isn't. It is just sometimes intellectual energy flows through her body, and that happens rarely. When it happens, you would want to listen to her attentively. So, when I had asked her about it, instead of instantly answering me, she asked me what a passion means for me? Well, this was an admirable way to approach the problem. I told her that passion is the thing what every successful person say that we should follow our passion and no matter whichever speech you listen to, you'll get the same advice to find your passion, and follow it with your heart.

Then she started to explain that passion is not anything big. She proceeded with the example when we start to see a TV series and we find it so much interesting that we forget every other thing we were involved with, and the only thing goes in our mind is a desire to know what might follow next in the TV series, and then our mind only wants to see more of the series. No matter if this series has 12 seasons or 5, we would see every episode to complete the series to know what happens in the climax. What would we say to this madness? We are passionate about it, aren't we? We don't see any other thing except this series. Have you realized that you could become so passionate about this series before you had started to watch it? When you gave time to the first episode of the series, you may have found out how much interesting it is. She continued that this is the same situation with our desires as well. We find something interesting, and start doing it for a few days, then we become bored with it. And it doesn't mean that you don't have any passion. Instead, it means that the thing you were doing wasn't meant for you. And again you try to search for new things, and that's how you came across the thing that can drive you crazy and maybe we can say then that doing this thing is your passion. And after this amazing example, she told me that living life without a passion is no fun, and it's boring. I have asked her many other questions, but she has a habit to not answer all of my questions, as I ask a lot of questions. That's all from her.

Till now, we can say that passion is an emotion. When we try out new things in our lives, it generates within us. Passion is just an emotion. Living without a passion is totally okay. Even if there's any question arises in how can we find something that can have this emotion attached to it? Is it really necessary? Well, to me, it is not necessary to have any passion to live a life.

Definitely, having a passion for only one thing is a way to limit ourselves in living only one aspect of our lives. If you will tell the people about having no passion, you'll definitely get strange stares, and it is totally okay. Because it is your life, and you have the right to set your own standards. If you don't like to have any passion, that's your choice. But is it true that you can have a boring life without passion? Umm, tough question, and I have an answer. NO, you will not have a boring life if you will not have any passion. Surely there are hundreds of ways to entertain your life and make it worth living.

You might be curious about why you couldn't figure out your passion. If you are like me, then I guess you don't like to restrict yourself, and not limit your possibilities. You like the idea to be boundless. But why everyone has their passion figured out?

I would like to assure you that it's okay, it is their doing that made them figure out their passions. It doesn't have anything to do with you. They might be the most logical ones in their life, and you seem like a creative soul, and it's really not easy for creative people to settle at one thing only. Read about Leonardo da Vinci. He didn't settle at only one thing as well. But will you ever be successful without a passion? Well, that depends on you. I would say yes, you can be successful without any passion if you'll do your karma accordingly.

Passion is an emotion. You can't have any feeling towards anything that was not yours, or something that you haven't done it before. You wouldn't get to know whether something is capable to generate this emotion within you, without trying it first by yourself.

The main problem is that people have given a lot of importance to finding this passion in their lives. It has become a buzzword nowadays. No matter who is it you talk to about your future, everyone would be giving this advice to follow your passion. And when you ask them about their passions, well, same as you, they haven't figured it out yet. People are ready to give free advice to anyone around, even without asking, and even if they hadn't tried it with themselves. These kinds of people don't have experience with the advice they happily share with others, and it's purely intellectual, and here the problem occurs. Because they don't understand the intricacies which arise during implementations of the advice that they are sharing happily.

We think that we can be passionate about only one thing in our lives. It is what this world talks about a lot. There seems a tacit rule of the world that we can have only one passion in our lives. It makes it even difficult to find our passion. Because it gives a sense that have to stick to the same thing for our whole lives. It makes us afraid to choose one thing as our passion because we don't like to limit ourselves. Imagine, doing the same thing for our entire life. That sucks to even think about that. I don't believe that we can be passionate about only one thing in our lives. The tacit rule of the world about passion doesn't fit in my life.

It is my pleasure to break this rule. I think we can be passionate about everything around us if we are willing. Well, after writing this much on passion. I don't want to have any passion in my life. It's funny, isn't it?

So how can you have many passions? How can you be enthusiastic about everything? The answer to these questions is simple. Go and get yourself involved completely in whatever you do throughout the day. Don't judge anything, don't filter anything into if it can be your passion or not.

Whatever is your task to do, do it with full involvement, be aware of what you're doing in a moment, be conscious about each and every movement you make, feel the movements through your whole body. When you cook, observe how it is turning from raw material to a tasty piece of meal that you and your loved ones will have. When you talk to a person, look into their eyes, look how their head moves, how their expressions change, their smile, wrinkles, where do they keep their hands and what message are they conveying subconsciously through their body language. Who knows, you might get to know them better. Anything you do, do it with complete involvement and awareness.

At first, it might seem hard to do. Many times we are being involved with our mind that it is not an easy task to be conscious of our acts. We may be sitting in a class or a meeting, but our mind is wandering to the shore of beaches or in the mountains. And it's not an easy task to get it back from the mesmerizing places. Sometimes, things aren't going well in our life, and our mind keeps us busy there instead of letting us focus on the present moment. I accept that what I am telling you to do might seem impossible at first. I might be telling you to do a lot. And it is okay to feel that. Don't overwhelm yourself in thinking how would you do it. Don't stress yourself. Don't think too much. Don't worry, you'll be able to do it. You just need to know how to start to incorporate it into your life. Just like I had started this in my life.

Start with one or two things at first to get completely involved with. Be it taking a shower, eating, conversations, walking, exercises and anything. Just start with one or two things to be completely aware of while you do it. Take your time to get used to this method, and slowly and graciously let it happen. Don't give a damn about whether something is your passion or not. That thought will stop you from doing anything. Don't look for passion anywhere, it'll come to you and if it doesn't come then know that you're a limitless being and passion can't reach you because of your limitless nature.

Be hundred percent involved with anything you do. This way you don't have to limit yourself to only one thing for the entire life, and you will be limitless. I like the wings you have on your back, don't let anyone cut it, fly high because you deserve it.

In this chapter, we have learned that passion is a kind of emotion. Passion is not required to live a happy and successful life. There is no need to define if anything is our passion or not. We can be passionate about almost everything in our lives if we are willing. There is no need to limit ourselves to only one thing in life. We are humans, we may be limited through our physical nature, and at the same moment, we are limitless when it comes to our mind.

Embrace your limitless nature.

FEELING LOST, HOPELESS AND DEPRESSED

I am feeling lost, lonely, hopeless and depressed. What should I do?

Getting lost in life can be overwhelming and frustrating at the same time. You can't find which way to go. No matter where you start, you always end up in the same spot. It is hard to see what lays ahead on the way. There are tons of thoughts showing you tons of things to do. You can't do any of it as you can't find a way to do all of those at the same time. You don't know where to go now. It is making you lose hope in almost everything. You have started to lose interest in the things that you found interested once.

You can't understand why this is happening to you and why now. You have tried to talk about it with your family and friends. Somehow it seems like they don't understand or just couldn't put themselves in your shoes to know how you are feeling. They are in a hurry to give you solutions instead of just listening. Because deep down you know that you've solutions of all of these problems in your life. You just want someone in life with whom you can share your true feelings. You don't want to be judged about it. You want to share it with someone who will listen to you without giving any piece of advice and just listen. Your relatives and friends aren't like the ones who can just listen to you.

It is giving you a sense of loneliness. You are feeling all alone in this world, even with your loving friends and family, who would do anything to make you happy. But still, you are feeling lonely once in a while these days. It really sucks to be like that. It really sucks to not be able to share the struggle you're going through.

Living in this world, being updated with the trend, you might be thinking that you're depressed. And now, you think that you're going through a depressive phase, and you have to go through it alone. Without any external help. You think that yeah it is real, you feel depressed. So you put a smile on your face to go out in this world, and at the back, you keep on assuring yourself that you're dealing with this in the best way possible. Many times, you think no one knows the struggle you are going through as you have hidden it successfully. And you still hope that someone should notice the pain behind that smile.

Might be possible that your friends and family doesn't know ways to penetrate through your happy face or they are too busy in their own lives with the same problems as yours. You have expectations from people around, and definitely, those expectations are not going to be satisfied because no expectation does.

So you're feeling lost, lonely, hopeless and depressed. Emotions that you're feeling right at this moment, need to be dealt only by you, and no one else can remove these things from your life.

Remember, you're the creator of your life.

Are you really depressed or is it just what new in the market is? What happened to your hopes? What is the thing that triggers loneliness in your life? If you carefully observe, you may know the exact reason for feeling lonely. As Newton said, "Every action has an equal and opposite reaction." Emotions are also generated by some actions in your life. Be aware of your actions and what emotions it generates within you.

So, whenever you feel lonely, just investigate what caused it. By knowing the root of this, you may find the way to deal with it.

"Losing the path is the only way to get it"

If you want to find yourself, then you would have to get lost first. I think you're in the right situation and on the right path of self- discovery. Understand that there is nothing wrong with getting lost in your life. It is completely okay. Not everyone gets the chance to get lost in life. Many people in the world have all sorted out. Only you, me and some like us got lost.

You have done very well till now, and I am sure you will do great from now on as well. It is when we get lost, we find miraculous things on the way. You might have heard of inventors and scientists who were working on something else and they invented something better. By getting lost on something else, they found better technologies.

Once it happened in my life. When I got totally lost, and I was lost in life many times, but this one is special. I got an admission in one of the reputed colleges of the city. Then at the university, second counseling was about to happen. Some of the new friends that I had made in the college, told me that in the second counseling we could change our college to another one which according to them, was better. So, I told my father regarding changing my college, he didn't like it, but he did the required paperwork. I had to visit the university with the papers and ask for the college change there. I was ready to go to another college with my new friends. I went to the metro and traveled to the nearest metro station to the university. That was the second time I was visiting the university, and I didn't remember the route clearly. And I didn't want to waste my money on rickshaws because I knew it was only a walking distance away. I liked to walk a lot.

I saw a guy walking in front of me, he seemed like a college going student. So I started to follow him. The path seemed familiar so I kept on walking for like a kilometer or so, and then when I reached the end of the road, I didn't see the university. Instead, I saw another college, and I was right about that college going guy after all.

Then I realized that I had to take the right turn from the metro station, and instead I turned to the left. So, I was lost there. I started walking back to the station and then turned to the right route towards the university. I went there, the second counseling had already started. I was late, but they let me in.

I sat there and gave a thought for a few seconds regarding switching to another college. My college was reputed ones in my city, and the one I was about to change to was similar, but it was far from home. Before giving my papers to anyone there, I sat and just thought one more time about it. I got up, came out of the room, straight back home. Now, when I think of that moment, it gives me chills to imagine what if I had given my papers to change my college. My life would have been different. I got lost, and somehow I realized that I didn't want to change my college, my friends did, not me. I was under the peer pressure. Now when I think of that moment, it makes me see that getting lost can be a good thing if we give ourselves time to be found again.

When we don't find any path to go to. It is natural to feel hopeless. When you try to talk to someone about your life, you feel like they don't understand you. And then you decide not to talk to anyone else about it. But deep down you still wish if someone would be out there who can listen to you without giving you any solution and just listen without judging you. In turns, it makes you feel lonely in the world full of people.

Loneliness doesn't mean that it can only happen to you when you're lost and hopeless or depressed. It can also happen when you're totally fine. Because there are always going to be some things in your life that you only want to talk to someone special. Those moments can make you feel lonely as well. It doesn't matter if that is your boyfriend or girlfriend, family or friends or colleagues or maybe your pet. If you don't have that someone special on whom you can trust with your deepest secrets, you don't have to stress about that either. It is also fine.

You know when all of these negative feelings come together to you, it can turn into depression as well. But these days depression has become like a cliché, everyone is thinking that they're depressed only because they didn't pass the exam, or are going through break up. Are you also thinking that you're going through depression? If yes, then you need to analyze yourself to know if you're really depressed. You need to be sure if it is not a mood swing of yours.

Depression is a disease that can happen to anyone. It needs to be dealt with on different levels at the same time. It affects our body and mind together. So, it has to be fought on both the warzones i.e. body and mind. It requires that a proper medical, physiological and psychological treatment is required to win over this. To fight depression, you need to talk it out to your elders or anyone around you as soon as possible. No matter how foolish or weird it seems. Because it is a dangerous disease and it can only be fought together, not alone.

So how can you know if you're depressed or just sad, well you're still reading this book. It simply means you're not that much depressed as much as you thought of yourself. You have hope to improve yourself. You are still finding ways to become a better version of yourself. You haven't given up yet.

And that's how I can tell you that you're not depressed and just going through a mood swing due to some emotional events happened in your life recently. That's all, nothing to worry about. You are improving yourself, and that's what matters.

Although, if you have been feeling constantly low for a longer period of time now, let's say if it's already more than a month or two, then it would be best and safe to take some outside help.

Whenever you feel lonely and can't find anyone to talk to, just pick up a pen and a notebook, start to write whatever comes in the mind. It doesn't matter how stupid it seems to you, and don't make any meaning out of it. Let everything flow out of your mind, through your hand, to the notebook. Keep writing until you start to feel lite. Don't put that pen away until you finish to get every shit out of your mind. Once you finish writing, you will feel lite, relaxed, peaceful and calm.

It might be possible that you don't like to write much. It is okay too because I have another way for you to take that shit out of your mind. Try to soliloquize. Stand in front of the mirror, give yourself a smile and start talking to yourself about the stuff in your mind. Instead of just standing there, you may walk and talk to yourself. Don't just talk in your mind, use your mouth and have a conversation with yourself. Just talk and talk, until you emptied your mind, until your mind becomes peaceful and calm, just keep on talking. You will feel lite. You have just talked to the person you can trust for your entire life, the person who will never leave, that is yourself. You may find it stupid, but it will work.

During my college, I wanted to improve my English. I talked to my friends about it. I tried to convince them to practice English speaking together. Some agreed to improve their English with me. We decided to meet at 9 am every morning for the practice. But no one stuck to the plan. On the first day, only 2 out of 4 showed up, and that day went by criticizing others for not showing up on time. Other two never showed up for the practice. On asking about the reasons, they told me that they couldn't wake up early due to which they couldn't come. It was one hell of a reason, we decided the timings mutually. So, months passed by and no practice happened. Nothing.

I was looking for the help, and they didn't come to the practice. I didn't give up. So I thought about finding people on the internet to practice English speaking. I found very amazing people to begin my practice with. Due to the different time zones, it was difficult to manage time and be available for the practice. So we were not always be able to do our practice.

One fine day, my cousin told me to try to talk to myself in front of the mirror to practice English speaking. He told me to talk about any movie or anything that happens during the day, and only speak in English. I started doing it, and slowly my speaking skills started to improve.

Days went by, I didn't know when I stopped talking about movies, and started to talk about my own life's problems. I used to come to home from college, and talked about anything that shouldn't have happened or about something beautiful like my crush at the college. So, time went by, and as I kept on growing, I had improved my English and found someone to talk to when there would be no one to listen to me.

I realized that sharing problems with others didn't give me any solution, but talking to myself gave me many solutions. I had even started to walk home from the metro station, and kept on talking to myself. It worked amazingly all the time.

This is how I had myself away from feeling lonely. Because I know that the feeling of loneliness only arises when we don't feel connected to ourselves. If we are connected within ourselves, then it is impossible to feel lonely at all. If there is a disconnection within yourself, then no matter how much trustworthy people you know, no one can help you with the loneliness part. You will always feel lonely even when you are around the people who loves you the most in the world.

To connect with the world, you need to find a connection within yourself first. So, spend some time with yourself without any distractions. Just you. Listen to what your body and mind telling you, before answering to anyone else. Try not to scroll down more in your social news feed. Make a balance between your offline and online lives.

In this chapter, we have learned that emotions are the result of our own actions and reactions towards our lives. We are the creator of our lives. We can control how we feel. We might not be depressed as much we think of ourselves. It could be our mood swings as well.

Depression is a disease, and it requires professional and personal help to fight with it.

Whenever we feel lonely, we can start to write or we can soliloquize.

When the connection within us is strong, we can never feel lonely.

Getting lost can be the greatest thing that can happen in our lives.

Let's move on to the next chapter to know simple things that can make a big difference.

SIMPLE THINGS

"Only great minds can afford a simple style." ~Stendhal

When you go through a stressful situation in your life, it may make you so frustrated that you might find every simple thing full of complexity. You see your life as a complicated happening. Even you keep your relationship status on social networks as 'complicated,' because it is cool to have that. It doesn't even have to do anything about your reality, even if you're single, but you want your status on social networks as 'complicated.'

Complexities and complications are in fashion nowadays. It has become a fashion to take a simple thing, twist it, stretch it and then welcome it in life. And then try to find someone who can come into your life and make all these things simple again, with all of this work, also gives you unconditional love. You might have seen people putting statuses on their wall or as stories so that you can read those statuses and know how much complicated their life is.

These days everything is complicated in your mind. Your relationship with your friends, family, parents, colleagues, neighbors and anyone you connect with during the day, is complicated. You can't even explain your relationship with your "just friends" to anyone, as there's only one word to explain it, and it's complicated. I see my friends going on dates, and when I asked them, they tell me that they're just friends and nothing more or it's complicated. I don't know why even a simple thing in your life has to be complicated.

To wake up on time in the morning, you use a lot of alarms. You put an alarm at 5 am, and then succeeding alarms after every 10 minutes, 5:10 AM, if that failed to wake you up, you've got another backup alarm at 5:20 AM, and so on after every interval of 10 minutes till 6 AM or maybe 7 AM or 8 AM. When you know that you won't be able to wake up at 5 AM then why put the alarm at the first place. Why are you disturbing your sleep by doing that? Also when the simple alarm clock doesn't work, you would try to find a new alarm app that gives the guarantee to wakes you up. Hence, you're complicating your life. Because a simple act of waking up, you have made it up as you are in a warzone with your sleep after every 10 minutes. And people from up above the stars are betting on whether you would wake up at the first one or the last.

Now, how complicated the life you've made up. It is easy to wake up at whatever time you want to wake up without an alarm.

You want to know how? Well, it is simple. You need to know how many hours you sleep every night. Let's say you need 7 hours of sleep at the night. You want to wake up at 5:30 AM. Then go to sleep 7 hours before the time you want to wake up i.e. 10:30 PM. Your body will be awake at 5:30AM without an alarm, with full restfulness. And you won't have to suffer horrible sounds of your alarm. You'll get the peace of mind, and you'll be more calm and relaxed.

When you wake up and start using that phone of yours. You don't realize, but you're filling your mind with shit. You're killing your mind's ability to think and be creative. You're not allowing your mind to be awake fully. You haven't even given your mind and body to get in sync with each other. The most important part of your day, you have given to the people who really don't care about you. By not giving proper time to your body and mind to be awake, you have increased the risk of having a bad or less productive day. It might seem like very little thing in your life. There have been researches about the negative effect of social networks on our brain. The time when you could have planned your day, you've wasted it. I know it is not easy to fight the temptation to check the updates in your phone the first thing in the morning. To check who missed you last night while you were in sleep, who has texted you, and you have to give them immediate response otherwise they would have to wait long. It is totally okay.

Understand that people will be fine without getting your reply, even if they are your loved ones. And definitely they must be doing their morning stuff as well, at least don't disturb them. Don't ruin their morning. Do this for the people you love, help them to be productive in their lives as well.

Same things happen when you're about to sleep at night. The phone doesn't let you sleep. You just keep on scrolling the news feeds of your social networks and putting shit in your head. I say it shit because it is shit. It really doesn't have much significance in the way you experience your life. You keep on chatting even when your eyes are heavy, but you can't just stop texting because if you do, you are afraid that your loved one will leave you. Well, if you can't even trust your loved one, then there is no need for your relationships. Break it.

Remember this "tomorrow starts with tonight."

Before you go to sleep, stop using your phone at least 20mins before and turn off its internet and Wi-Fi, so that it won't buzz while you sleep. Read a book for some minutes. Lie on your bed with your eyes closed, and think about how well you've spent your day. What you could have done better. Think of it as a day retrospection.

A perfect way to start the day as suggested in our culture, and have been transferred through our dadis and nanis. When you will be awake the next day, before opening your eyes, just rub your hands and put your palms on your face, giving yourself some warmth. Then roll to your right side and get up slowly. Give a big smile for you are alive today, and give another bigger smile for everyone else around you who is alive. You can use your phone to check time, but only when you don't have a watch at home. Don't use your phone until you have a nice breakfast. Shhh... it's a crime to use phone just after waking up.

Bring some kind of exercise in your life in the morning. It could be lite exercises or some lite yoga or some simple stretches. You don't have to do all the exercises or yoga asana. You can choose an asana such as Surya Namaskar, yoga namaskar, and any other asana. Do it for a complete mandala. According to yogic science, the body goes through a certain cycle every 40-48 days. When you do a yogic practice for a full mandala, you'll see a significant changes within you. Don't worry about it for doing it for the complete mandala, you can try it for at least a week, and you can observe the changes within you.

After doing exercises, take a nice and cold shower, then you can start to plan your day.

Have a big and nice breakfast.

Now, you are ready to deal with the world.

When you will start to do all of these little things, you can see that your body and mind will say thanks to you for doing it.

Bringing these little changes in your life can have significant effects from day one.

I wish you the best and fly high.

CONCLUSION

Life is a struggle. We heard this a lot, be it in movies or in reality. Many of us think that life is nothing but a constant struggle. Have we questioned this prejudice that is forced upon us? Did we try to examine this well-believed stuff?

Since our birth, our mind is constantly getting feed up with all the beliefs that our parents, grandparents, neighbors, friends, and relatives have. Unknowingly, we made others' beliefs into our beliefs as well. Without questioning anything out of that. No matter what kind of shit it is. We don't care or dare to question.

When we were a child, we used to be excited about everything around us. We were curious for every drop of water, everything that we come in contact with. Most importantly, we were aware of our surroundings, living in the moment. It didn't matter what happened in the past nor were we worried about our future. We were happy and content.

Figuring out how things work was used to be our one of the favorite things to do. Why Sun always set in the west? Why does rain happen? Why are some people angry about little things? We have lost the ability to question the beliefs thrown over us. We are living with problems in our pockets. Instead of facing those problems, we tend to make ourselves busy. We are afraid to deal with the problems head on. Although, how small the problem it may be. We don't want to face it. We want everything to be fixed with the magic wand or maybe with a snap. We pray for everything to be alright, and we don't want to do anything ourselves. We want some kind of energy to work for us. We want to find our passion because then an emotional energy will drive us and we don't have to force ourselves into doing any actions. We had made ourselves believe that our life is nothing but a struggle.

Life is many things but not a struggle. Life is a joy in itself. Life is the present that we got. Life is there in smallest possible creatures and the biggest creatures as well. In the wilderness, you will find that there are many beings with enormous physical strengths and a huge memory records. Being born as a human on this planet is a marvelous opportunity. Because there is no limit to our mental power.

We are limitless. Through the limitless power of the mind, we can create our life in whichever way we want to. We are the beings on this planet who have realized that life isn't only a survival but it's much more than that.

Just being aware of our aliveness is enough to make our lives from a mere struggle to a limitless bliss.

In this book, we learned that our mind needs to be in a state of relaxation to live the life as it is. We learned to realize the smallest pleasures – like that of having each drop fall on our body. We learned to pass our thoughts on the paper which helps to clear the mind. We learned to get lost in our own world to give ourselves the refreshment our mind need.

We learned to accept the consequences of our doing in our lives. We learned to take the responsibility for our lives in our hands. When we change our perception about our life, karma, and its results. It gives us the mindset to do something about our problems. When we realize that this is all because of our actions only, then and then only we can work something out to solve the problem. Then and only then we will be ready to take the responsibility for our own life. Most importantly, we got to realize that we are the creators of our own, and we can make our lives as hell or heaven that depends on us.

We learned that to find solutions for any kind of problems in our lives. We saw that asking the right question can give us the answers we are looking for. No matter, if we are confused to take a big decision in our lives, asking appropriate questions to ourselves, can help to find the way to the right decision. Even the fear of any kind cannot come into our path if we question the fear. Just asking the right question may vanish the fear in front of us.

We learned the importance of time and the present moment. We learned about our mortal nature. We were reminded that we are temporary and when our time will be over, we won't be here anymore. Without any advance notice, anything can get vanish from our lives. Everything is temporary here. Time will pass one way or another. It is we who have to decide what we want to do with the time we are given. Live life as a struggle or as a joy, what will it be with you?

We learned that passion is a kind of emotion. To live a happy and successful life, it is not required. There is no need to define if anything is our passion or not. We can be passionate about almost everything in our lives if we are willing. There is no need to limit ourselves to only one thing in life. We are humans, we may be limited through our physical nature, and at the same moment, we are limitless when it comes to our mind.

We learned that emotions are the result of our own actions and reactions towards our lives. We are the creator of our lives. We can control how we feel. We might not be depressed as much we think of ourselves. It could be our mood swings as well. Depression is a disease, and it requires professional and personal help to fight with it. Whenever we feel lonely, we can start to write or we can soliloquize. Getting lost can be the greatest thing that can happen in our lives. When the connection within us is strong, we can be lonely.

Bringing little changes in our lives can bring tremendous transformation. We need to learn to respect small things in our lives. We need to stop ignoring the smallest signs that our body and mind is giving us. We have to be aware of everything.

Let us be limitless for once and for all.